Although he has written extensively on political a
this is Anthony Coombs' first foray into books. H
do so by Bobby and Bubba themselves. Whilst rel
Alexander for their everyday needs, they insisted that "grandpa" Anthony
use his dwindling literary skills to share with the world their "irresistible
charm" and the adventures it gets them into.

In any spare time Anthony gets from dog walking, he combines
a career as chairman of a FTSE finance company with building houses
and overseeing a charitable trust which supports children and young
people with physical and mental disability challenges.

Following his earlier incarnation as a Member of Parliament,
Anthony also likes to write about current affairs. He loves both football
where, despite his father once owning Birmingham City, he is an avid
Aston Villa fan, as well as the fancy footwork required in ballet where he
sits on the board of the Birmingham Royal Ballet.

Anthony likes to torture himself at golf, more gently in the gym
and to take equal care of his soul as a practising Christian and trustee of
Premier Christian Media.

Most important of all, he is the proud husband of thirty-eight years
to Andrea, and of course the father of B&B's daddy, Alexander.

Bobby and Bubba's SMALL ADVENTURES

Anthony Coombs

ILLUSTRATED BY
Adam Share

SilverWood

First published in 2022 by SilverWood Books
Paperback edition published in 2023

SilverWood Books Ltd
14 Small Street, Bristol, BS1 1DE, United Kingdom
www.silverwoodbooks.co.uk

ISBN 978-1-80042-251-3 (paperback)
ISBN 978-1-80042-197-4 (hardback)

British Library Cataloguing in Publication Data
A CIP catalogue record for this book is
available from the British Library

Page design and typesetting by SilverWood Books

Bobby and Bubba would like to dedicate this book to
their "A" family of Alexander, Andrea and Adam…and Michela
and all those who make their lives so happy –
particularly their pampering friends at Love My Human.

Bobby and Bubba

Bobby and Bubba's small adventures – a warm welcome from the two boys

Hello! Our names are Bobby and Bubba Coombs and we are brothers. Our parents, Alexander and Michela, say that we are British bulldogs; they stress the 'British' because there are now so many more French bulldogs in London than there are of us. But they hope that something called 'Brexit' will change that.

Most of the time, we all live together in Chelsea right in the middle of the city. Although the houses are beautiful and the streets pretty clean, there aren't many green and grassy places you can go to run around and sniff. (Sniffing is our favourite hobby.) Still, we are allowed out every day so long as we wear a harness to keep us safe from the traffic. The traffic is noisy, gets up your nose and will hurt you if you run into it. As well as our harnesses, when it's cold we wear 'shooting jackets'. Smart or what? The rest of the time we live in a big rambling house in Warwickshire. Then we don't need harnesses but just spend our days running about the fields, sniffing and licking the grass and, of course, sleeping. Bliss!

Of the two of us, Bubba has a bigger body but is really the goodie, goodie. On the other hand, Bobby, or Bob, is the mischievous one, who loves any adventure without ever thinking where it might lead. Bubba, meanwhile, likes his bed, his bone and, most of all, cuddling up to his parents on the sofa or their bed…but he does have a temper.

We are very lucky dogs. We have masses to eat, comfort galore and the cuddliest family in the world. We fight all the time but never hurt each other. Everyone says we have a dog's life and are spoiled rotten, but that doesn't mean we haven't got our eight paws on the ground and our noses just as close.

The countryside is great but London is home. It's beautiful but can be a very cruel place. For dogs, that can mean being abandoned on the cold hard and wet streets of London before the lucky ones get rescued by the Battersea Dog's Home which is just across the park. For humankind it can mean sharp elbows, honking cars and rushing about without really seeing anybody else. Often human*kind* it's not.

But London is still home. Every day we go out to stroll, sniff and savour it. Nearly everyone likes to stop, to chat and pat. It's amazing what you see from a foot above the ground. That's where the sights, sounds and smells of London really are, and why they lead us to so many adventures. However mischievous, sometimes disobedient and often naughty we might be, that's what makes the world so wonderful.

So, come and join us on our walks of discovery!

1

Bubba, Bobby and the Tramp

Just like the trees in Marguerite Terrace, which Bobby and Bubba usually 'watered' on leaving home, Alfie was a regular stop on their walks around Chelsea. Styling himself a 'gentleman of the highway', Alfie seemed to live on a bench on Dovehouse Green, although, since it was only feet from the King's Road and reeked of petrol, no one really knew why.

One morning at the beginning of summer, Bobby and Bubba were chasing their ball on the green – or at least as much as their harnesses, on the other end of which was Michela, would allow them. It didn't take long before Michela was so entangled in knotting leads and swirling dogs that with one big heave...over she went on her bottom. A cackle of laughter cut through the Italian expletives.

"You alright, darling?" Freed from his bench, Alfie shuffled over with a big smirk on his wrinkly face. Bobby ran up to him and to the fascinating smells issuing forth. Michela wasn't so impressed and leapt upright. Armani Prive and Street Aroma don't go well together.

"I'm fine. Thanks." Bobby and Bubba crowded around the old man, panting and wagging.

"They're so strong," sighed Michela.

"Let me hold one while you get yourself together, doll," Alfie offered, taking hold of Bobby's lead.

"That's so kind," Michela replied dubiously. But Alfie beamed like he'd been offered a big pork chop. Bob and Bubba stood there gazing at his bedraggled face.

He gazed back. "Beautiful, ain't they? Smashed up faces look a bit like mine…" Another cackle was drowned out by the King's Road.

"Come on then, boys," declared Michela as she grabbed Bobby and then hurried away without a backward glance.

One week later, Bobby and Bubba were back on the Green, this time with their number one daddy, Alexander. Alexander was the human they loved most of all, but that didn't mean they listened to him very much. So, when they saw Alfie lying on his bench, they dragged Alexander over, wagging and shaking with delight.

Bobby was just about to launch himself into a bout of licking and affection, when…

"Bog off, you two," Alfie snarled – at least that's what it sounded like, muffled as he was in his shabby old blanket. "Can't you see I'm not very good?"

"Sorry, Alf." Alexander pulled Bubba away from his enthusiastic licking of the huddled man. Just as he did, he caught sight of Alfie's face – the bloodied welts on his cheek and the deepening bruise around what used to be his eye.

"Bloody hell, Alfie," he blurted. "What on earth happened to you?"

Bobby and Bubba sat like stones, stiller than they'd ever sat before. Bobby cocked his head. Neither had seen blood before and it made them twitchy.

"Bit of sport for the World's End boot boys and their posh mates," said Alfie. "Didn't like me making me bed on their park bench."

"Bullies!" muttered Alexander. Bobby and Bubba weren't meant to hear and didn't understand when they did. Alfie's eyes were sad. Alexander looked angrier than they'd ever seen him before.

"Well, you can't stay here like this, old fella. Got to get you cleaned up and looked at." Alexander's huge arms lifted Alfie from his bench as if he was a child. Bobby and Bubba followed on their best behaviour...no sniffing and no pulling.

And then Bubba had a moment of genius, led as usual by his nose. There was something about the smell of Alfie's clothes which reminded him of a place he used to pass on the King's Road. He began barking like he'd never barked before. He stood, motionless as a rock, staring at a building up the street. Suddenly he began to pull. When Bubba pulls, it's like a tug dragging the *Queen Elizabeth*. The Ivy, Natwest and Chelsea Town Hall seemed to fly past as Bubba dragged the little posse in his wake.

Bubba was headed for Boots, two hundred yards up the King's Road. "Come on, you two," he barked.

Bobby and Bubba were suddenly on a mission of mercy. Obedience personified. They led Alexander along, then sat outside the shop either side of Alfie, like two solid bookends either side of an ancient collection of papers.

Minutes later, Alexander emerged with a bag smelling of carbolic and antiseptic. The little procession continued on its way when, a hundred yards on, it was Bobby now who thought he remembered something...like an old biscuit down the back of the sofa...but he couldn't think what. He suddenly stopped and stared across the teeming road. Bubba did likewise, bringing Alexander to a screeching and slightly irritated halt. Then the penny dropped – and Bobby started barking. Bubba wasn't sure why but joined in anyway. Bobby came to a halt at the door of the Methodist

Church, and at a sign which rather unimaginatively read, 'Glass Door'. Alexander studied it too. "Isn't that the local homeless shelter, Bob? You are a clever boy." Bubba and Bobby's tails went into overdrive – or would have done had Bubba ever grown one.

"You OK, mate?" Alexander asked Alfie, rather foolishly in the circumstances. "Can't clean you up here in the street, but these two seem to have come up with a rather good idea..."

So, off the little procession stumbled, one of Alexander's arms around Alfie's bony body and one holding his worldly possessions. Bobby and Bubba now didn't need their harnesses and they carefully led the way straight into Glass Door, whose smells had jogged Bubba's memory into action.

Musty, sweaty but sweet, the winey odours inside would stay with the boys forever. Kindly and capable hands took Alfie into a side room while Alexander explained to the young volunteers what they had seen, how they came to be there and Bubba and Bobby's part in it. "Good boys" was the signal for a frenzy of patting, cuddling and licking, laced with biscuits and treats for Bubba and Bob, the heroes of the hour...and a glorious brew for Alexander.

Twenty minutes later Alfie emerged shaken but calm, bandaged but unbowed. "He can have a bed here for the next few nights," the man from Glass Door said, "but after that it's up to our useless social services or he's back on the streets."

"Well, he isn't going there," declared Alexander to Bobby and Bubba's delight. "I'm no Good Samaritan but we're not letting Alfie out of sight until we find him a roof over his head."

So that's how Bobby and Bubba acquired their new best friend, occasional house guest and regular walker and companion. Like most things in life, they couldn't solve Alfie's problems, but they could certainly lighten his load. Alfie did eventually find a roof to call his own and even a job to keep himself.

And, you know what, it brought them all – Alexander, Alfie, Michela and, of course, Bobby and Bubba – more happiness than any of them could ever dream of.

*

2

Bobby, Bubba and the Angel

Bobby and Bubba weren't big into religion. Although their grandpa, Anthony, went to the Old Church in Chelsea every Sunday morning, Bobby and Bubba's own parents, Alexander and Michela, usually stayed in bed. Sundays, much like every day, were generally devoted to eating, playing, walking and sleeping rather than to God.

Which was a pity. For although Bobby and Bubba loved Chelsea and most of the people in it, they noticed things. Their walks smelled of fag ends, were littered with discarded crisp packets, and their paws were often sticky with pavement chewing gum they couldn't avoid. Even worse, Bubba once stepped in a bag of doggy 'unmentionable' which had just been dropped in the street. He wasn't allowed in the house again until he'd been hosed and disinfected…

But sadly, it went beyond this. More and more, Bob and Bubba noticed little things which seemed to sour the milk of human kindness. The ever longer blasts of car horns; the finger in the air from cyclists running a red light; Bobby once even saw some local lads barging a lady as she stepped into the newspaper shop.

Another time, Bubba couldn't understand how a mother leaving school slapped her little boy in the middle of the street! More and more, people seemed to be living in little 'bubbles', too much in a rush to even look at, far less talk to, their fellow humans. Covid-19, masks and social distancing only made that worse.

As Bubba once remarked to Bobby, although it wasn't exactly Gotham City out there, the rough edges of uncaring seemed to be seeping everywhere and into everyone – sometimes even into their own family.

One day, Bobby and Bubba were at their grandparents' house ready for a walk. Andrea and Anthony, grandpa and grandma, weren't arguing but the boys noticed that, after fixing their harnesses, they weren't exactly walking close together. A chill was in the air.

Although it was early May, all the budding leaves of kindness and generosity seemed to be absent from the trees. For the umpteenth time, Anthony was moaning about what he unkindly liked to call Andrea's 'Little Book of Resentments'. Bobby was being brought up sharp with "Wait!" and Bubba was continually being dragged away from rather interesting smells in the box hedges of Christchurch Street. The milk of human kindness was souring, and you could almost smell it.

The toxic little party had just reached the front doors of Christ Church itself and were turning the corner. Anthony was just about to launch yet another bad-tempered salvo, when Bobby noticed a thin, ragged creature, with straggly hair and a hoodie pulled over an old Chelsea football shirt.

As this creature was hurrying past, suddenly its voice rang out. "Be kind to her mate – you're meant to be a gentleman," he said in a broad cockney accent. Anthony was just about to tell him to mind his own business when the words died in his mouth. He, Andrea, Bobby and Bubba were frozen in their tracks and they gaped after the retreating little figure. The oracle had spoken.

Before anyone could regain the power of speech, the oracle had disappeared. For all of them, time was suspended like an intake of breath.

"Well," sighed Anthony at last, his head throbbing as though he'd been struck by lightning. He turned to Andrea. "I'm so sorry, beauty. I'm being an absolute pain. Please forgive me."

Thunderstruck, Bobby and Bubba looked from husband to wife and back again.

"He was dead right, though," Andrea replied.

Just then the church clock struck midday. Although it was a Sunday, during the Covid lockdown all the churches had been closed.

Even so, it seemed that God had found a way to send His message of kindness and love to a family and to a world much in danger of forgetting it. It didn't need a sermon, psalms or a church service. Just Bobby, Bubba and their grandparents out for a walk. The world felt refreshed.

Of course, the supernatural aura wore off quickly. The boys were soon off again, pulling and scrapping as usual. But they did notice that the sun had come out and that Andrea and Anthony were suddenly holding hands again.

3

Bobby Coombs, Dunce or Genius?

Sometimes two people seem to live in the same body. While Bubba was a sensible dog, a little plodding but gentle and consistent, Bobby wasn't. Although around an inch shorter than his brother, Bobby had Napoleonic traits. They certainly didn't include consistency.

Bubba loved Bobby very much but, like everyone in the family, found him very difficult to understand. For Bubba, a good day was usually the same as the one before but for Bobby, happiness was always something new, vivid and exciting.

Usually this revolved around anything that was moving. A car leaving the long drive at Cedar Lawns in Warwickshire was irresistible. A cyclist in a London street just had to be chased. Most of all a ball wasn't just an object of fascination but of total obsession… Whenever a ball was thrown in the air, the lights went out in Bobby 's head and switched on in his little eyes. Nothing – not even his beloved brother – could separate Bobby from his quarry. Little Bobby just lost all control.

It sometimes happened when Great Grandma, aged ninety-three, came for tea.

"Careful, Bob," warned Andrea when she arrived. "Great Grandma's skin is very thin – you scratch her and she'll bleed."

Two minutes later, up jumped Bob to give Great Grandma a kiss.

"No! Bobby! Get down! You're just being silly again."

But it didn't stop at silly. Bobby used to like to take a nap on their

daddy, Alexander's bed. One afternoon he was dozing... and slipped away into a beautiful dream. He and Bubba were out for a walk; the sun was shining; the air was cool, and the bushes and trees were SO inviting – especially for a dog who hadn't been out all day...

Bobby awoke – but not in the garden. "Bob! You dunce!" It was Alexander shouting this time. "You've wet my bed! What the heck are you doing?"

Despite the most appealing face he could muster, Bob realised Big Trouble had landed.

Appropriately enough, Bobby was in the doghouse. Everybody was looking down on him... The idiot child... Brainless Bob, the canine clodhopper.

But was he really? Ten days later, Grandma Andrea (the same one who had given him the ticking off over the bedroom incident), was working out on her cross trainer in the gym. As usual, although a little unsure as to what was being 'worked out', Bobby and Bubba were keeping her company.

Bobby was having a little nap, but it was constantly being interrupted by the whining and bleeping of Andrea's high-tech machine, as it reeled off information on her weight, body fat level, calorific output and even life expectancy...as well as making her sweat.

At last Bobby had had enough. Creeping around the back of the machine he found the little wire which fed electricity into Andrea's noisy contraption. He didn't need to chew it – a little tug, and the machine coughed and spluttered…and blissful silence reigned. Andrea was so dumbstruck it took her a few moments to break the sudden calm.

Glancing around, she saw Bobby beaming up at her. "Bob! You are a naughty boy! I nearly fell off my machine – but what a very clever one! Whoever taught you to do that?"

News of Bobby's electrical genius spread swiftly throughout the house.

"Perhaps he's – a genius savant," proffered Anthony. "Bob, we all thought you were so stupid – and now you're dismantling the cross trainer!"

Was Bobby a genius or a dunce? He couldn't be both. Or could he? Bubba didn't know the answer, because there wasn't one. Like most people and their furry friends in this world, Bobby was neither one nor the other. 'Stupid' or 'genius' were simply labels which changed from day to day. They didn't scratch the surface of who Bobby really was. Deep down, like all of us, Bobby was a little enigma and that's why Bubba loved him with all his heart – and always would.

4

Bobby's Dreams

Bobby and Bubba love sleeping. Or at least that's what it looks like, since they do it at least ten hours every day. Most of the night they slumber close to each other in their beds on the floor; sometimes they wrap around each other, or at least as far as their rotund little bodies will allow their brotherly love to go.

The rest of the night is spent snuggling their daddy, Alexander, who loves the warmth and trust Bubba brings, and who likes sleeping even more than they do. Bobby, on the other hand, is more of a flibbertigibbet, twitchy, adventurous and the lightest of sleepers.

Which brings us to dreams. We don't know exactly what went on in Bobby's head but recently, Michela, his mummy, had noticed that Bob had begun barking in his sleep. Of course, Bobby couldn't explain exactly why, since although he always woke himself up, he couldn't ever remember what in his dream he had been barking at.

Whatever it was, it must have been following him. On their walks in Battersea Park, he would steal glances behind him, as though something was following him and nipping at his tail.

It can't have been very frightening since Bobby had always been very sensitive to sudden noise, even a passing bicycle bell, but he didn't seem bothered by this. All the same the pattern continued. Snoring soundly… a little bark…eyes opened, a long stretch and then back to sleep again.

Nevertheless, Bobby's habit of glancing behind him on his walks did seem to be getting worse. In fact, Bubba was getting worried that Bobby was in danger of doing most of his walks backwards and hitting lamp posts, other dogs and baby prams on the way! Otherwise Bobby was his usual appealing self, drawing legions of adoring passers-by on his perambulation around Chelsea.

Then, late one evening in the boys' country house in Warwickshire, the secret of Bobby's dreams was revealed. In January, although the days were lengthening, by five o'clock when Bobby and Bubba went out for their pre-dinner walk, it was dusk turning to dark. As usual they were on the wide front lawns, sniffing the grass and borders and 'baptising' them to mark their territory. Bubba was in the lead investigating the sounds of approaching night, as the stars rose, and the shuffling rustle of country wildlife brought the undergrowth to life.

It was then Michela saw it, a nanosecond before Bobby did. Ten yards behind them, a black shape, a little smaller than Bobby but lithe with luminous reddish eyes, was following them.

In a trice, Bob whirled around to confront his tormentor, tearing towards it with the deepest and most ferocious growl his little body had ever produced. What Bobby intended to do beyond growling thankfully remained a matter for debate, since the black cat turned tail and shot up the nearest cedar tree, snarling and hissing.

Bubba then joined his brother in sitting at the bottom of the tree and barking his head off too.

The cat vanished. Bobby felt the hairs running down his back gradually subside, and, after all the adrenalin, a feeling of great peace

and resolution came over him. Bubba got up and nuzzled him but, though he was grateful, he really didn't need reassurance. For that was the very cat, seen once when he was just a puppy, which had roamed his dreams.

"Good boy, Bob!" shouted Alexander as he led the boys back to the warmth of the house. "You really showed him off, didn't you? Proud of you!"

And in truth Bobby was a little proud of himself too. For those vivid red eyes and charcoal coat had been haunting him in a way he simply couldn't explain. But now instead of running away from the spectre or just trying to live with it, he had been brave, and had turned to face and confront his fears.

As the great American poet, Robert Frost, once observed, "The best way out is always through." Bobby, for all his bravado, had been frightened – but fear is the source of true courage. And Bobby had proved it.

5

Bobby, Bubba and the Accident

It was a grey and dank November day. The kind of day when it was never really going to get light and when even a fur coat and a flask of coffee couldn't keep out the seeping damp. It was a day for an accident...

Even Bobby and Bubba couldn't wake up properly. Usually, the words 'walk' or grandpa Anthony's less coherent 'Wiggy, wiggy, wiggy' would see the boys hurtling towards the door. But today it only produced a kind of leisurely trot, as though they were suspicious of the very air itself in the cold outside.

Andrea felt the weather more than most. "I can't stand this country!" was her opening jibe. "Sodden, never any sunshine and dreary beyond belief."

Bubba could see that this walk wasn't exactly brewing as cheerful, as the little party trudged in silence past the tennis courts and the old cottage garden, nodded at Antoni the Polish builder, and then squelched through the beautiful gate he had just built into the quagmire of a field, which in spring would be a meadow.

As always, Bubba and Bobby were looking on the bright side. The grass tickled their tummies, the soaking blades were a delight to lick and chew and the old tennis ball, balanced in 'Covid's' antlers (Covid is a deer made of branches, and old iron built by Adam the artist during Lockdown) at the foot of the old oak tree, promised biting, fighting and fun.

But, that day, fun wasn't meant to be. Apart from a few weary throws, Bobby and Bubba's human companions didn't even sit down on their usual bench for a chat. Rain was spotting, clouds were scudding, and gloom was everywhere.

About ten minutes later, the dreary troop mercifully reached the gate separating the orchard from the garden lawns. They then headed for the little knot garden with its formal narrow path and neat box hedges. They halted at the heavy oak door which led to the lawns at the front of the house, and the trees which gave Cedar Lawns its name.

Andrea paused. "We ought to teach the boys to wait on command. Let's see if they will actually sit until I let them go through to the other side."

"Sit!" was duly ordered and Bobby and Bubba knew exactly what to do, despite positively vibrating with expectation at the prospect of the juicy lawns on the other side of the door. Gingerly, Andrea unlatched and slowly eased the massive door open.

Bubba and Bobby quivered as though heaven itself lay on the other side of that door. Inch by inch, the little gap in the door widened. "Stay," Andrea warned. "Staaaaay…"

BANG! The naughty couple catapulted, Bubba headfirst flying through the door and knocking Andrea flat onto her back and into the low box hedge beside her.

"Naughty boys!" shouted Anthony, only to be drowned out by Andrea's juicier epithets as gloom spilled over into fury.

But the gods had not had their fill just yet. Leaning over, Anthony took Andrea's arm to pull her to her feet. As he did, the iron latch of the heavy oak door swung towards her, slamming into her head.

Andrea screamed and fell back, blood pouring from a cut just above her right eye. Bobby and Bubba, the guilty parties, crept back to the scene of the crime looking very sheepish indeed. A gloomy day had now imploded.

Of course, swathes of dressings, litres of antiseptic and gallons of soothing reassurance couldn't put that Humpty Dumpty of a day back together again. Bobby and Bubba were banished to the doghouse, with muttered and multiple threats – all of which ended with 'the dogs' home'.

The two brothers retired to their beds, next to each other as always, but now in deep sorrow, and even deeper disgrace. Bobby, ever the philosopher, tried to reason why this terrible accident – which would

require two doctor's stitches in Andrea's beautiful face the following day
– had happened at all.

"Whose fault was it, Bubba?" whispered Bob. Bubba had really
rushed first but it was Bobby who had caught Andrea's leg and sent her
sprawling. Or was it Anthony? He actually pulled Andrea onto the door.
(He definitely bore the brunt of Andrea's first screams.) Or did blame lie
with the wind which blew the door at the very worst moment? Or was it
even the door itself?

Bubba's head whirled. There'd been an accident and hurt. An
inquiry was needed. Someone had to take the blame. But then Bubba
had an inspiration. Was all that *really* necessary? Granted, they HAD
been naughty. No, Bobby and Bubba should not have rushed to that door
but…they hadn't meant to hurt Andrea at all, just as Anthony and the
door and even the wind were innocent too.

Perhaps blame and guilt – and even forgiveness – were just sticks
to beat ourselves with. Maybe, as the Buddha himself taught over two
thousand years ago, they were actually sometimes signs of a selfish
inward-looking view of life.

So, Bubba consoled Bobby, "Don't worry – sometimes accidents just
happen!"

Despite our rage and need to investigate, to hold to account, to right the 'wrong' and even to punish – very often, actually *no one* is to blame. After all, that's precisely what we mean by 'accident'.

6

No Pulling! No Jumping! Bobby and Bubba's Lessons on Time

Bobby and Bubba love their walks. As soon as he sees a harness, Bubba, in particular, is like a canine tank. If the door wasn't opened, he would probably charge right through it, with Bobby clambering after him.

As usual, today the boys hit the road as though the clock was ticking to the end of time itself. Dragged onto the pavement outside, Anthony, Bubba's grandpa, began his rather plaintive cry. "Bubba! No pulling!"

Even when accompanied by a sharp tug on his harness, this appeared to have no effect on Bubba at all. In fact, like swotting a wasp, it seemed to fire him up even more! Off set Bubba and Bobby, dragging Anthony and Andrea along like a sleigh without snow.

"Not so fast! What's the rush?" This was simply met by even more pulling, stretched arms and straining harnesses.

For Bobby and Bubba were in a hurry – even though they weren't sure why. Maybe it was the lure of the lamp post – especially if you've been cooped up since breakfast. Perhaps they could smell the grass in Burton Court Park, where balls are thrown in abundance and the children shriek and play. Or perhaps it was the people they would meet – a growing legion of Bobby and Bubba fans who love to pat them, ask their ages, tell them how beautiful they are, and generally be totally captivated by their legendary charm.

It happened all the time – at least twenty times in an hour's walk.

Bobby and Bubba like people and, as usually happens, people like them back. Although the boys had no idea why, today they were hurtling towards Pimlico. There lay Daylesford, famous for its delicious smelling meat, and where Andrea could actually find a coffee during lockdown.

As Andrea went inside, Anthony collapsed onto a bench. "Bob, Bubba – I'm exhausted! We don't like dogs that pull! You pull, I hold on and we all end up feeling like we've fallen off a cliff!"

As usual Bobby wasn't listening – he was far too busy playing court to the host of admirers, their children and other dogs who bombarded them with, "Aren't they beautiful? Such great colours! Are they brothers? How old are they? Where can I get one?"

Bobby got very excited indeed and the friendlier they got, the more he got excited. "No jumping!" was Anthony's despairing plea as Bobby greeted an elderly and elegant couple. The lady was wearing a very glamorous beige cashmere coat…sadly beige, and Bobby's muddy paws were not a great look. "Oh boy!" was all Anthony could think to say, as Bobby leaped up for a kiss.

"I'm so sorry," Andrea said, returning with the coffee. "I'm afraid they've never worked out the difference between friendly and overwhelming."

Happily, the elderly lady was kind, as deep down she knew Bobby and Bubba to be, and hurried on her way.

Bobby and Bubba's unending *joie de vivre* didn't just end at jumping. Even more chaos was waiting just 100 yards down the road on the other side of the iron railings, which separate Royal Hospital Road from the park at Burton Court. There, a little spaniel puppy – no more than four months old – was chasing an old tennis ball. As soon as it spotted Bobby and Bubba, over it came. A game of licking and sniffing through the rails quickly ensued. What Bobby and Bubba didn't realise was that iron railings didn't protect tiny spaniels at all. In fact, King Charles puppies were small enough to wriggle through…which is precisely what our new little friend proceeded to do.

Bedlam! Anthony tried to grab the tiny creature before it ran into the traffic, at the same time frantically heaving on Bubba to stop him following suit. Seconds seemed like hours, but at last Andrea caught the little dog and gently squeezed him back through the bars, whence he had come, and into the arms of his parents, nearly paralysed with shock.

Bob and Bubba ambled off wholly oblivious to the near tragedy their enthusiasm had caused…but the frozen silence, tightened leads and quick march back home promised an Hour of Reckoning when they got there. For Bubba, who was really a loving and responsible dog, knew that pulling on the lead was naughty and wore everybody out. Bobby didn't quite get that, but anyway was feeling rather bad about the lady's cashmere coat.

So, the telling off they walked into a few minutes later wasn't entirely a surprise. But after the expected admonitions against being naughty and disobedient, Anthony came over all philosophical.

"If there's anything I've learned during this pandemic," he said, "it's to slow down and to smell the roses. Don't judge life by what might – or might not – be just around the corner. Whatever you boys do, do it carefully and in your own time. No need to rush! Good things find their own time. As a very wise man called Mahatma Gandhi once said, "Never judge the quality of life by its speed."

Bobby and Bubba looked at each other and nodded off to sleep.

7

Bobby and Bubba Meet the Children

Bobby and Bubba were growing up now – or at least growing out. Although only two, like most British Bulldogs they resemble bodybuilders and weigh in at between twenty-seven and twenty-nine kilograms each. Bobby is all shoulders while Bubba is built like a tank – but still, inside their heads, they're the sweet little boys of their puppyhood.

That can lead to misunderstandings. One such occurred one day in Burton Court, which is a park with a football field, cricket square, tennis courts and a play area near their home in Chelsea. Although a little snooty – entry by members' card only – most people there are as friendly as their doggie companions…with very rare exceptions.

That Sunday was just one of those. Bobby and Bubba were taking Andrea and Anthony for their walk. It was a dry grey October afternoon, and the boys couldn't wait to get off the pavements in Chelsea and on to the soft wide-open grass of the park. At least, in part, this was the legacy of Bobby's sore paws, of which, perhaps, there will be more another day.

Happy, loving and friendly though they are, Bubba and Bobby tend to combine a little tactile over-enthusiasm with an excessive interest in any moving object – a passing car, a bicycle, a scooter or a giggly laughing child.

While Bubba isn't really that bothered, Bobby reacts exactly like Pavlov's canine friend…and then his brother joins in. That day the park was reached, their harnesses dumped and, like a bird uncaged, off Bobby and Bubba romped.

Their first friend was a black Labrador who sniffed a lot and smelled great. Just around the corner of the football pitch, up trotted a poodle – female, pretty, alluring – completely beyond Bob and Bubba's life experience. The boys lack of any romantic sensitivity then led to the kind of appalling behaviour usually reserved by humans for at least a third date.

Fortunately, a strategically-thrown tennis ball soon provided much-needed distraction and off they raced.

Bobby and Bubba are fascinated by children, who play with the same booming energy that they have. More so when the objects of their intended affection are so inclined to laugh, shout, and run giddily about. That's the kind of chase and play game that Bobby and Bubba find irresistible.

At first, all went well. Bobby sniffed and wagged his little tail and Bubba ambled around. The children stroked, and a little licking and patting were exchanged. Then one of the children started laughing and shouting. Bubba replied in kind by jumping up and licking. Unfortunately, when twenty-seven kilograms of Bubba collides with six years of small infant – one falls over…and Mummy becomes hysterical. Off streaks another child who tumbles over to a similar bout of horizontal licking.

By now laughter has turned to tears, parental indulgence to indignation. Bobby and Bubba are bewildered. How can play and affection turn to shouting and anger?

Back in their harnesses and with the children back gibbering in the indulgent arms of their mothers, calm returns – although recriminations continue.

"Why can't you keep your dogs under control?" "Those dogs are dangerous," were two of the unkinder phrases thrown at Bobby, Bubba and co as they made a swift exit from Burton Court.

All were now very sad on a very quiet walk back home. The last thing they wanted their 'play' to do was to frighten or upset. But why were young humans allowed to run about, and shout and scream, when

Bubba looked at Bobby. "Perhaps it is time to look in the mirror and see ourselves as the children see us. We're not exactly pretty, are we?"

Bobby blossomed into philosophy. "Yes, however kind you mean to be – sometimes you have to try very, very hard to prove it."

8

Bubba is Forgiven

Bobby and Bubba spend *all* their time together – in fact, they can't remember ever being more than twenty feet apart. If they spot anything of interest, they're off like a couple of bullets – tied by an elastic band. They sleep together, eat together, fight together and lick each other clean whenever they get bored.

Despite all that, they are very different. Bobby finds noises startling, while Bubba is sleepily phlegmatic. Bobby is a smaller but more inquisitive

dog – Bubba is cuddlier and more affectionate.

As a duo, they are adorable – but they don't always get on, usually when the ownership of a bone or a ball is involved. Bob regards all spherical objects as his by God-given right, so that on rare occasions, when Bubba actually gets possession, he holds on for dear life.

One day, Bubba had a bone in his mouth and was sitting on the top of the steps leading to the lawn in the big house in Warwickshire. When Bobby approached for a nibble, Bubba growled. Bobby grabbed; Bubba held on, and a tug-of-war began. Closer and closer to the edge of the veranda they slid… Suddenly, Bobby tipped over, let go of the bone and fell four feet onto his back on the hard shale below.

Out rushed Cecilia, the housekeeper, to help Bob gingerly back to his four feet. For once, Bobby was quiet and Bubba – now being scolded by Andrea as "a greedy boy. I saw you growl" – was crestfallen.

Bobby tried to climb the stairs again, but after failing to make step two, was carried by Daddy Alexander into the house. There he lay, feeling very sorry for himself and with a badly twisted leg.

"Naughty boy, Bubba!" Up went the cry. Bubba shuffled away feeling ashamed of himself and very down in the dumps.

The vet lived just three miles away so Bobby was gently lifted into the back of the car, where he couldn't really move but bathed in all the attention and in the warmth of Alexander's lap. Back at home, Bubba looked miserable – never before had he been parted from his brother. Was he badly injured? When would he see him again? Would he ever be forgiven?

Bubba slunk to his bed next to the lobby and waited…and waited…

An age passed, the light faded and then the doorbell rang – voices, lights – but where was Bobby?

"They've had to give him a general anaesthetic to examine him," said Andrea. "We'll see how he is in the morning."

The morning? thought Bubba. There's a whole night to get through before then!

Bubba and Bobby had never, ever been parted for a night, and usually slept in their beds a foot apart at most and often in the same one. Bubba rolled over onto Bobby's bed and moaned. He didn't want his dinner, a new bone, or even his evening cuddle with Daddy Alexander. All he wanted was Bobby. It would be a long night.

And so, it proved. When Cecilia opened the door to let Bubba out the next morning, the poor dog was a bit of a mess. He hadn't really slept. He kept imagining Bobby was just an inch away at the foot of his bed, and couldn't get rid of the knot in his stomach. That's why he didn't eat breakfast and just lay on the stone floor, facing the door through which they carried Bobby, in what seemed like an age ago.

Another hour passed and Bubba kept pricking up his little ears whenever he heard the magic word "Bobby" from the kitchen. About midday, at last Alexander and Andrea pulled up on the drive. Bubba shot out of the back door.

The door of the car opened and there was Bobby being gingerly lowered down by Alexander with a bandage around his leg – Bobby's not Alexander's.

"Torn ligament but no break," announced Alexander, as Bobby hobbled to the door. When he saw his brother, he tried to hobble even faster, but the effort was too much and he collapsed in a heap. Bubba was all over him, licking and wagging and barking and happier than he'd been in his whole short life!

"Be careful, Bubba," advised Alexander. "Bob is going to need a lot of rest."

Then Bubba trotted off to the kitchen and rustled around until he found what he was looking for. Back he came with a beautiful new bone

– and gently, and almost reverently, he put it into Bobby's mouth.

After that, he just lay down next to him, with love and relief pouring out of every inch of his body. He snorted slightly, and fell asleep.

9

Bobby and Bubba Meet the Snake

Although they like life in London very much, Bobby and Bubba always look forward to staying at their home in the country. There they have the run of the big house, although they aren't allowed into any room that is 'white'. This means most of the bedrooms except their daddy and mummy's and – very strictly – not the sitting room where everybody watches TV, and where all the furniture comes from California.

Even more fun are the gardens and fields: brimful of sounds, smells and fluttering creatures, which are always a little too fast to catch. That doesn't stop Bobby from trying, particularly in a corner of the big front garden when he suspected a rabbit family lived. He became aware of this when he came across a rabbit which was very still and dead. Definitely the dirty work of the feral cats who live nearby, he and Bubba thought.

One day, Bobby and Bubba were out with Andrea and Anthony, for what they called a 'constitutional' – a walk around the grounds usually accompanied by a flask of coffee. They eventually sat down beneath the boughs of an old oak tree which, in the early summer, was surrounded by long meadow grass and butterflies.

Bobby and Bubba didn't drink coffee, but they did like to play-fight, especially over any object round enough to qualify as a ball. Bobby's eyes always glazed over when he saw one, and he got quite manic in chasing and harrying it. Because the grass was about twice as tall as he was, he often lost the ball and, very often, himself too.

Coffee and conversation duly completed, Andrea and Anthony's constitutional continued on its windy way until, about ten minutes later, Bobby and Bubba reached the rickety and gnarled farm gate leading into the orchard.

Usually losing yourself in the grass – at least for a short while – wouldn't matter, but recently there had been reports of snakes spotted in the cottage garden. This garden was a beautiful Edwardian space filled with sweet smelling plants and bushes, which, with a little help from Alistair, the gardener, had the glorious habit of disappearing completely every winter and miraculously re-sprouting every summer.

The report of the snake, however, may not have been very reliable, since the lady who spotted it became hysterical…and a fortnight later managed to vanish completely – the lady not the snake.

Anthony creaked open the gate and, forgetting their manners as ever, Bobby and Bubba rushed into the orchard for an apple, pear or plum – although most were too sour to eat this early in the season.

Suddenly Grandma Andrea screamed. Bobby and Bubba had found a new toy to play with; this one was about three feet long with vivid yellow and orange V shaped colours on its back. As usual Bobby and Bubba had allowed their overweening curiosity and wish to be friends to overcome their better judgement. Spontaneity had spawned stupidity.

The snake, whose bite would have meant at least a visit to the local vet, if not a fate closer to that of the rabbit, didn't want to play at all. Anthony and Andrea were now going berserk and shooing Bobby and Bubba as far away from the creature as possible.

In a flash the snake was gone and Bob and Bubba looked up reproachfully – they had lost a friend.

Maybe the snake was dangerous and didn't want to play…but Bob and Bubba weren't so sure, and now they would never know. Wasn't that always the human's purblind reaction to a creature they rarely saw? To recoil from it, control it and then with the weight of seven and a half billion of their kind, aim to capture and even destroy it? A simple creature who, in a gentler world, Bobby and Bubba, in their usual generous and kind-hearted way, might have made a playmate and a friend?

So, Bobby and Bubba had a tinge of sadness as they trekked back into the garden and its safe and well-tended lawns.

Bubba thought to himself: there's a place in the world for all creatures great and small – and not just those as cuddly as us.

10

Bobby and Bubba's Fighting and Biting

As animals grow up, especially in the doggie world where Bobby and Bubba live, they change. From tiny puppies you could hold in your hand, Bobby and Bubba are now nearly thirty kilograms each of solid muscle with an attitude to match.

That doesn't mean a change in character – they are still the lovable, adorable pranksters who attract fans in Chelsea on a scale Elvis Presley or the Beatles would have envied. But they have discovered 'testosterone',

a big word for what changes our bodies, as we – humans and animals – grow beyond ten years of age or about two in 'doggie years'.

Bobby and Bubba are there right about now. Their barks are deeper, they have the strength of Hercules and (much as they love each other) they see each other as competition. What used to be fighting, and even biting, and playing rough, has now – at just three years of age – become a new obsession, whether it's getting their food first, catching and keeping the ball or racing crazily through the nearest open gate, whatever the dangers lurking behind it.

Bobby and Bubba's country home in Warwickshire is next to a lane down which drivers seem to instantly metamorphose into Stirling Moss or Lewis Hamilton. Therefore, the gates leading onto it can be very dangerous indeed. Bobby believes that anything on wheels – bicycles, scooters, tricycles or even a Ferrari – has been specifically designed for him to chase. Bubba is only just behind him. In fact, being much faster over the 100-yard drive leading from the house, Bubba usually hits the gate first.

One day in late winter, when the lawns crackled with hoar frost and the snowdrops were peeping through, Bobby and Bubba were chasing an old tennis ball on the front lawns which, with the towering trees flanking the drive, gave Cedar Lawns its name. As usual, testosterone and rivalry were in the air, which meant that no matter who reached the ball first, fighting, biting and plentiful growling was sure to follow.

Like an old-fashioned wrestling match where no one ever really gets hurt but where someone just might, the 'fight' was stopped and the precious ball removed by Andrea, the referee. Which was a good idea but with very bad timing…

The oil tanker supplying Cedar Lawns comes once a month. Exactly at that moment it appeared at the gates. Andrea screamed to both Bobby and Bubba, and Charles in the house who had just activated the gate to let the tanker in.

"No – stay!" but too late. Slowly, agonisingly, the automatic gates swung open. Oblivious to the panic and chaos outside, the tanker driver slowly moved up the drive, with Bobby and Bubba snapping at the tyres as though at a giant mechanised bull. The gate to the lane yawned open behind it.

Mercifully, this patron saint of tanker drivers juddered to a halt and, before Bobby and Bubba realised it, the gates to Cedar Lawn were moving slowly shut.

Andrea, heart pounding and breathless, was merciless. "You *naughty* boy, Bobby," she bawled. "You could have been *killed*!"

Bobby's little face pleaded forgiveness and it was instantly granted. But Bubba's testosterone surge had the opposite effect. No sooner had the word 'naughty' escaped Andrea's lips than Bubba actually…GROWLED, and growled and growled.

Now, Bubba has always been the cuddlier of the duo, the big softie, the needy one, even like Lennie from Steinbeck's *Of Mice and Men*. Bobby, on the other hand, is the little Napoleon, independent, short, impulsive but sometimes curiously insecure.

But here was Bubba growling his handsome head off. "Leave him be," advised Anthony as Andrea shook her finger at the dog. "It must be the shock."

But was it? What had turned Bobby and Bubba's world on its head? Had a chemical reaction in Bubba's growing body triggered his brain? Or was he really frightened and simply defending himself and his brother? Or was he just being very naughty indeed?

We will probably never know. The world is an unpredictable place and, growing up in it, whether as a human or a dog, can be very complicated. Bubba has rarely growled since; he's still the one trying so hard to be 'a good boy', who licks Bobby's sore paw and cries when they are separated. But sometimes we can all do things which even shock ourselves.

Has that ever been you?

11

Bobby and Bubba's Big Break

Bob and Bubba aren't very fond of being clean. For Bubba, that too often smacks of antiseptic wipes in unmentionable places, which really sting. For Bob, it requires admitting that his regular habit of beginning a walk by smelling another dog's pee and then licking it off the pavement isn't terribly hygienic.

Anyway, thought Bubba, a doggie smell is a warm, furry and comforting one which shouldn't be lost in a wave of shampoo and carbolic. It's what makes a dog a dog.

But there is an exception. Bob and Bubba do love 'grooming'. Now that might sound suspiciously close to 'washing' and so it sometimes is. There is a mountain of water, suds, splashing and shaking to be performed before the real fun in grooming begins. This is when a glittering array of stroking, brushing, teeth and ear cleaning, liniment and paw potions is performed. Most of all Bobby and Bubba love it because, for a few very precious minutes, it means that they are COA – Centre Of Attention!

And where does this irresistible experience take place? About ten minutes' walk from their little house in Chelsea, just across the King's Road, in a shop called, with a hint of irony, 'Love My Human'.

So, one Thursday afternoon, accompanied by Andrea and Jack, the driver, Bobby and Bubba were trotting along the said road for that much loved – and needed – grooming treatment. As always, the welcome they received from Fran, Angelica, Robert and their boss, Susan, was

deafening and like the homecoming which, for Bobby at least
(being most susceptible to COA) it almost was.

Down they clattered on the stairs leading to the parlour, where
a bunch of equally pampered dogs were either frothing or barking before
treatment or emerging – Zen like – from that unforgettable canine
nirvana.

Bob and Bubba immediately got down to their usual routine
of sniffing, wagging and continuously impolite inspection of their
companions' private parts. They then settled down to await the Call to
Shampoo. The two brothers eyed each other, wondering who would be
first, and didn't notice the faint sound of snarling and snapping coming
from the shop upstairs.

"Bobby Coombs," came the summons and Bobby bolted for the
door as Bubba sighed, stretched and resigned himself to a boring wait.

It could hardly have been ten minutes before Bubba was invited to
join his brother in Groom Heaven. The cries of the girls greeting them
mingled with the happy barks of the animals being treated.

But the clouds were gathering over their little sunlit sky. Partly
because he was bigger, and mainly because he was more sensible, Bubba
had always 'big brothered' Bobby. That's why, while still halfway through
his treatment, out of the corner of his sleepy eye, he spied Bobby leaving

the room in a spasm of tail wagging and patting.

Now, although both dogs had the power and tenacity of little bulls, and a bite matched only by five other – much bigger – breeds, neither had an aggressive bone in their body. Whether it was a Labrador, a spaniel or more usually a fox terrier snapping or nipping, neither Bobby nor Bubba has ever been known to retaliate; they merely sought refuge in inglorious retreat without even a growl in return.

So, Bubba lapsed back into his soporific world of strokes, cuddles, pats and gentle probing as the doggie nurse went about her work.

Suddenly, the hairs on his back and the nerves in his spine snapped to attention. He could hear snarling, snapping and a bloodcurdling scream from the waiting room. He guessed that the scream came from Jeanette, the housekeeper, who had come to pick up the boys. Bubba hurtled from the bed, through the door and into the waiting room where he found Bobby cowering in a corner while an evil-looking bull terrier snarled and snapped his jaws at Bobby's head.

The combination of love for his brother, fear and anger catapulted Bubba into Bobby's tormentor with a roaring growl which must've been heard on the King's Road. There followed an explosion of mangled sounds which seem to last forever, but for about five seconds, as the bull terrier then backed away growling warily at the shocked group, visitors and assistants.

"Good boy, Bubba," Jeanette managed to pant at last. "Brave boy," as Bobby showered Bubba with licks and nuzzling while keeping a watchful eye on Bully Boy. Bubba's hair was still bristling, his hackles up… But his spirit was soaring as he looked at his little brother and at the small trickle of blood coming from his nose.

Bully Boy was hustled out and away, amid profuse apologies offered to Bobby, Bubba, Jeanette and in fact anyone else in the vicinity. "It's never happened before!" "So sorry – we had no idea he was so unpredictable," and "He won't ever be allowed in here again."

But it didn't really matter. Bubba's expression bordered on the beatific as he and Bobby clambered the stairs to be met by a chorus of grateful, adoring …and now respectful fans. Andrea rushed in and threw her arms around Bubba and then, more gently around Bobby. "*Good* boy! The best boy ever!" A small river of applause rang out on the proudest day of Bubba's short life.

But even better was to come.

"Boys," Susan announced, "I've got great news. Channel Four are doing a programme on doggy grooming and they apparently want two stars to front it. I can't think of a more wonderful choice than you two! How about it?"

Bobby and Bubba looked at each other and then slowly, and with a cocked look of enquiry on their faces, gazed at Andrea and Jeanette. "How *about* it? You *bet*!"

12

Bobby and Bubba's Best Day Ever... So Far

Bobby and Bubba never actually look for friends – but they find them wherever they go. A very wise man called Aristotle, who died over 2,000 years ago, once said that 'happiness is within ourselves'. Bobby and Bubba, as dogs so often do, simply exude happiness…and people everywhere feel that deep inside.

That's why it wasn't a total surprise when Bobby and Bubba found out they'd been pitched to 'star' in a television programme on grooming. The location was to be 'Love My Human', a doggy hairdresser and massage parlour all rolled into one, and to which the boys were absolutely addicted.

What was a surprise was that the bulldog breed – of which Bobby and Bubba were proud examples – had been selected for such attention. For bulldogs aren't exactly classically beautiful. They boast a lot of wrinkles and have faces that look as though they have just lost an argument with a brick wall. In fact, the British Veterinary Association recently thought their faces had become a little too flat for their own good! But since these were the only faces Bobby and Bubba have, or ever will have, they just went on living with them.

So, one Thursday, our two brothers could be found, harnessed and camera ready, trotting down the King's Road in the proud company of Grandma Andrea and Daddy Alexander. For this was a special occasion, evident from the spick and span-new paint glistening on Love My

Human's front door where they were greeted by Lucy, the shop owner herself.

"Bobby! Bubba! You look so handsome! Aren't they adorable?" A deluge of compliments showered the boys as they trotted in. How eager they were to reach the parlour, so much so that the producer cried:

"Hold it! Hold on. We'll have to go back to the door again to get another shot."

Bubba dutifully reversed direction but Bobby dug his paws into the floor and had to be skidded back along the newly-polished wooden surface. Take two was more successful. The two boys were soon into their full thespian stride, as cameras whirred and flashed, and canine egos were inflated to a potentially unhealthy size.

Half an hour later our two budding superstars re-emerged – together with an adoring cast of groomers and very decent footage of the whole experience.

Bobby was in his element, wallowing in the attention from a growing number of onlookers attracted by the lights and cameras spilling out onto the King's Road. Off they trotted into the quieter normality of London streets. Bubba had had a wonderful time too, but, as a sensible and down-to-earth dog, he had a flicker of worry in the pit of his stomach. Somehow all the attention, and the strutting and kissing, seemed a little out of kilter.

Bobby, on the other hand, was oblivious. Off they walked and eventually reached Sloane Square. Here they met Pala, their old friend from Armenia and a *Big Issue* seller, sitting quietly in his wheelchair – the legacy of an encounter with a land mine on his farm which blew away his legs, part of his arm and all his dreams of a peaceful, rural life there. As always, Pala greeted the boys with a smile and Bobby, in particular, pranced around, full of himself and dreams of stardom. As usual, Alexander handed Pala five pounds for the magazine offered to him. Bobby and Andrea then hurried away and Alexander turned to follow them. As he did, Bubba's lead almost jerked his arm off. Bubba sat there holding his ground in front of Pala and barking his head off. Rock still, Bubba quietened down but his soulful eyes moved from Pala to Alexander, to Pala's five remaining copies and back again.

"What on earth's got into him, Pala?" said Alexander. "He seems obsessed by your magazines."

"Maybe he wants you to buy some more for your friends," joked Pala. "I've only five left to sell today."

At this Bubba's ears lifted a little – as far as a bulldog's can – and his barking resumed and resumed and resumed. By now a little crowd had formed, and Bobby and Andrea had come back. Bobby looked at his brother and instantly understood.

Both sets of the world's most doleful and appealing eyes now fixed on Alexander. He looked at Andrea searching in his pocket for the twenty pound note he nowadays only kept for emergencies. Hesitantly he offered it to Pala.

"I'll take all five," he declared, as Bobby and Bubba leapt upon him in a frenzy of tail wagging, jumping and attempted licking.

Pala got the same treatment too as he sang out, "Blimey" What a nice man you are…and what dogs! If you hadn't done that, I'd have been stuck here in the cold for at least another two hours."

Their good deed for the day accomplished, Bobby bumped up to Bubba, whose knotted feeling in his tummy had now completely evaporated. Bobby and Bubba then led Andrea and Alexander back home with a spring in their step. Far more bouncy and carefree than any they had taken on leaving the film set, pumped up with indulgence and pride.

It dawned on them that while happiness may depend upon ourselves, true happiness is found in the little often unremembered acts of kindness to others. It was that, and not their new found stardom, which made this day their 'best by far'.

13

Bobby, Bubba and Dog

It seemed a doggie lifetime ago when Bobby and Bubba first met Alfie, the tramp. Since then Alfie was happily a tramp no more. Since the day that the boys and their daddy, Alexander, had rescued Alfie from the Kings Road bullies and taken him to Glass Door, the Chelsea charity for the homeless, Alfie had re-discovered his life.

A year later he had his own room in a clean and tidy hostel, a couple of mates with whom to discuss Millwall Football Club and even a small job as the caretaker/handyman for a couple of local parks.

Of course, Alfie had never forgotten his little fat bulldog friends and their daddy, Alexander. Bobby and Bubba may have come from the posh side of the Kings Road but, with their noses close to the ground and warmth in their hearts, they befriended Alfie for what he was, not what he had or where he had come from. They may not have shared the same colour, class, race or even species but they loved Alfie anyway. And in Alfie's eyes they were his mates.

Best of all, Alfie had found a new companion too. Actually, it was Dog who had found Alfie. Weeding one afternoon in St. Luke's Park, Alfie had spotted the mangy creature cocking his leg on one of Alfie's precious and newly-planted box hedges.

"Oi!" Alfie shouted. "What d'you think yer doing? You'll poison me box like that! Take a hike before I kick you into the street!"

Dog stopped, then moved gingerly away. But Dog didn't cower. In fact, he stood his ground when Alfie shuffled up to him and felt his neck for a collar.

"My lord, you're a strange one," Alfie muttered. "No collar. One blue eye and one brown…and thin as me garden rake. Now let me get on with me work." With that, Dog lay down, watchful as an owl, his eyes constantly on Alfie.

An hour later, dusk had fallen and Alfie was packing up. "Off you go 'ome then! I'm locking up now and you're getting in me way."

But Dog didn't move. He cocked his head and studied Alfie. For, as Alfie had once been, he was a Nowhere Dog: nowhere to sleep, no master to obey, no bowl of food, not even a name to call his own. So, it wasn't a surprise when Alfie left the park, crossed the street and looked down … to a black-and-white face with one blue and one brown eye.

After that, as so often with the best things in life, Alfie and Dog just found each other. It wasn't planned, and it wasn't even likely, but for two lonely beings without homes or family in an everchanging and anxious world, companionship just took root.

Bobby and Bubba watched the new bond grow, with an occasional nip, snarl or even bite as their reward– for Dog wasn't the easiest of friends. A life of loneliness and self-reliance had put him on his guard. He was suspicious of his own shadow and wary of his place in the world. Whilst Bobby and Bubba inherited a world of warmth, affection and security as very British Bull dogs, Dog was a mongrel, of mixed race, uncertain parentage and, until recently, of no fixed abode. Like refugees everywhere those things made him an object of pity, of curiosity and occasionally of resentment.

One summer day, the three dogs were back in Burton Court Park with Andrea and Jeanette . All was peace and calm and sunniness until, from across the cricket square, loomed a tall aristocratic figure. She had black hair, a haughty air and two sleek Afghan hounds with attitudes to match.

"Pardon me," the black-clad figure proclaimed. "Don't let your animals near my Bruce and Charlie. I don't want them smeared with the mud and grime you three seem to be caked in!"

Bobby, Bubba and Dog looked at each other and Bubba noticed

a glint of anger in Dog's eye.

"First, they're not at all muddy," retorted Andrea, "and, second, concentrate on your own dogs before bossing mine."

At this the black-clad figure halted, drew herself up and hissed, "At least mine are elegant and pedigree, unlike your two wrinkly mutts and their black-and-white nondescript friend."

Bruce and Charlie, the sleek and highly-bred Afghans, then made a very serious mistake. They began to growl and slink forward menacingly.

On any other day, Bobby and Bubba would have shrugged their massive shoulders and just ignored the woman and her Afghans and their horrid behaviour. But when they heard their black-and-white and loyal friend being called 'a nondescript mongrel' they saw red.

Actually, they saw black and white…for that was the colour of Dog as he rushed towards his snarling and growling adversaries. Heads down, Bobby and Bubba charged. Dog alone was no match for the Afghans but with a combined sixty kilos of Bobby and Bubba behind him, the outcome was never in doubt.

Bruce and Charlie took one look at the charging trio, turned tail, and fled leaving their aristocratic owner breathless and harrumphing as her precious thoroughbreds cowered by the cricket pavilion.

After allowing Dog and the boys the pleasure of a minute's barking and growling, Andrea whistled. "Off you come, Dog, Bob and Bubba. Let's go home!"

So off they tramped, the so-called 'wrinkly mutts' and their mongrel friend, heads up and spirits high. They'd seen off the prejudice, entitlement and sheer bossiness that too often masquerades as 'the establishment'.

A little battle had just been won – and not just against two large Afghans and their bossy owner. For, what the boys and Dog had really proved was that what counts in this world is not a matter of a common race, religion, breed or upbringing, but the respect, companionship and (whisper it to Dog) *love*, shared by friends.

Bobby, Bubba, Dog, Alfie, Andrea and Alexander are really proud of that.

14

Bubba Learns a Lesson

Bubba Coombs is a good dog. He loves his smaller, but feisty, brother Bobby as much as he loves himself. He always tries to be the very best boy he can be. If Alexander calls "sit", "dinner", or especially "walkies" Bubba always shows up first. Bobby, on the other hand, always has something more interesting to distract him – a ball or a bicycle or a wheelbarrow to chase.

But, like all of us, hard as he tried, Bubba can't always live up to the best of himself. Sometimes, it seems that Bubba tries too hard to be Alexander's "very best boy", to be the first for cuddles and for dollops of affection. Because Bubba, despite his size and fierce looks, is actually a very insecure boy. And that makes him jealous…

One day he was lying on his bit of Alexander's bed, with four paws in the air – his usual "tummy tickling" position – when Bobby bounced in.

In fact, Bobby didn't just bounce in, but crashed onto the bed almost on top of Bubba.

"Hey!" cried Alexander, as twenty-eight kilograms of British Bulldog landed on his delicate parts.

Out of the corner of his eye, Bubba could see his annoying little brother enthusiastically licking his daddy; his own idyllic "tummy tickling" session had just screeched to a halt.

So, when Bob jumped playfully towards him, Bubba growled – not just a murmur but a deep, angry fighting growl, followed by a snarl and a snap which nipped Bobby in the face!

When Bobby took exception to this and snapped back, a cacophony of snarls and whirling fur followed as the boys wrestled on the bedroom carpet.

"Oi!" shouted Alexander , as he leaped from the bed. "No fighting, you *naughty* boys!!" Alexander grabbed Bubba's neck – under which Bobby was barking and struggling. Then, Bubba made one of the biggest mistakes of his life…

He whirled round, snapped at his daddy and then…actually bit him!!

"Oi!!" shouted Alexander again. "Bad boy !!"

Alexander retreated, holding his wounded hand as blood began to seep from it. The shock silenced them all. Bobby and Bubba stared at their daddy, and Bobby shuffled away slightly from the scene of the battle.

"What on earth do you think you're doing!?!? How dare you bite your daddy?" Alexander glared at Bubba, whose lower jaw jutted more like Churchill's than ever before. Bubba glared right back…and then made his second biggest mistake ever.

Looking straight at Alexander, he moved closed and growled again – deep and menacing. Bubba followed this up with what looked suspiciously like a snarl.

Alexander, who had a temper of his own, was astounded. In fact, he was outraged. "Behave yourself, Bubba," was his quiet but menacing warning.

So, when Bubba growled again and went to spring, thirty kilograms of bulldog was met by a fist on the end of 120 kilograms of Daddy Alexander.

Alexander had never smacked either of the boys before. So Bubba didn't yelp, although his nose hurt a lot. He certainly didn't cry, because that's not what British Bulldogs do. But he *was* in total shock. He stared at the daddy he adored, with his mouth open and a little dribble coming from the side.

Alexander was stunned too. He felt he had done the right thing because, after all he had done for Bubba, all the loving and cherishing, he knew Bubba needed to be taught a lesson.

Love and cuddles were a two-way street, after all.

Bubba would always have love and affection. It didn't even have to be earned. But what Alexander did demand was love and respect in return. And it wasn't just about feelings – actions also counted. Growling certainly wasn't included on the 'acceptable' list, and nor was biting.

Bubba slunk out of the bedroom and down the little back stairs which led to the kitchen.

Bobby didn't quite know what to do. Torn between loyalty to this brother and love for his daddy, he just sort of sat there and vibrated.

Meanwhile, it wasn't just Bubba's little nose that was sore. Lying in his bed next to the boot room, he was miserable and forlorn. Not just because he'd been naughty and had hurt the person he loved most in the world, but because he had let himself down.

All that time and effort trying to prove to his daddy that he was a good and obedient boy had just vanished in a trice.

A little tear formed in the corner of Bubba's wrinkly face and he sighed...

Being sent to his bed as a punishment didn't just affect Bubba, however justly he deserved it. Life isn't that simple. For Alexander, despite knowing that he had done what was right, was also wracked by guilt. He too had hurt his soulmate, companion and the animal he loved most in the world (equal, of course, with Bobby) and that made him very sad too.

But, as the Bible teaches, the greatest of all gifts is love. Love overcomes all – even though it might take a little time.

That's how, over the next few weeks, sadness gave way to forgiveness; forgiveness gave way to goodness and, eventually, goodness to joy and lots of cuddles and kisses – and, of course, tummy tickling.

The boys and their daddy had all learned a lesson and were family once again.

15

Bobby and Bubba and the Boy

Bubba opened one eye. It was still dark and very quiet, apart from the soft sound of Bobby , snoozing next to him. As usual, although they each had a bed, Bobby had snuggled in next to Bubba during the night.

Bubba could hear a robin chirping happily away outside; Robin was always awake before Bobby and Bubba.

Bubba knew that Bobby would be awake soon and then it wouldn't be quiet anymore.

Bubba thought how much he loved Bobby even though he could be pretty irritating. They had been together for as long as he could remember. Suddenly Bubba felt a little sad. In the beginning, there had been eight of them – four boys and four girls – but now it was just the two of them.

Bubba was curious about what had happened to his other brothers and sisters. Where were they ? He remembered that they had all left one by one. He knew that he and Bobby were very lucky to have been chosen by Alexander, their human daddy.

Bubba wondered if his brothers and sisters ever thought about how much fun they had even before they had names. Eight tiny pups without names.

Bobby's left paw wriggled and Bubba knew Bobby was awake. Big yawns and lots of grunts came next... and then Bobby was wide awake. Bubba could see immediately that Bobby had been planning things for today.

Things had been disappearing from the garden shed. First, it was some of the apples from the orchard which were stored in big barrels before they became homemade apple juice. Then there was the old basket with all the blankets, and last night Bobby and Bubba overheard Alexander saying that all the eggs had gone missing. Ruby had laid six eggs but, when he went back to collect them, they had all disappeared! However, Bubba knew Bobby would have a plan.

It was still early. Alexander was cooking bacon and eggs and, hopefully, a few sausages which were Bobby and Bubba's favourite. They ate their breakfast quickly as they were eager to get out into the bright morning.

Out they scampered through the long grass in the fields to the shed. The door was closed, but Bobby knew where the cracks were and how to wriggle in.

Bobby stopped suddenly and listened. There was snoring coming from the shed. Loud, loud snoring. Bobby and Bubba were puzzled. This was not dog snoring. This was human snoring, similar to Alexander, their daddy.

Bobby wriggled through first and then Bubba. It was very warm inside the shed and, in the corner, there was a big pile of blankets - Bubba recognised them as some that had gone missing from the house a few days ago. The snoring was coming from underneath the pile of blankets.

Bubba barked once. There was no response. Nothing. Just more snoring. He and Bobby began barking together. Suddenly, the pile of blankets moved and a tousled head of dark brown hair appeared. An eye peered at them.

Bobby and Bubba enthusiastically introduced themselves – and that was their first meeting with Mo, their sixteen year-old new lodger and friend.

They discovered that Mo had been living in the shed for a few months. He had run away from the orphanage where he had grown up, and decided he liked living in the cosy shed. It was peaceful and quiet, and there was lots to eat from the garden and orchard, including the delicious eggs. All that and the scrumptious apple juice, meant he was very happy.

Alexander came to meet Mo and heard his story too. He took Mo up to the house so he could take a big bubble bath. Then he gave Mo some new clothes, and set about finding jobs for him on the farm. Alexander said Mo would be paid a wage, and could have all the food he needed, as well as a proper bed to sleep in, and a room all to himself.

Bobby was happy, but he thought Mo needed just one more thing – a best friend, like he had in Bubba.

Suddenly his little ears pricked up and Bubba saw that Bobby's little tail began to wag. He had an idea…